Who's Looking?

How Animals See the World

Carol Matas

illustrated by
Cornelia Li

ORCA BOOK PUBLISHERS

IF YOU WERE A LITTLE BABY, EVERYTHING COULD LOOK LIKE THIS.

Babies are born with very good vision, except for one thing—they can see you clearly only if you are close to them! Anything else is just a big blur. At first they see mostly in grays, but soon they start seeing bright colors such as red.

IF YOU WERE A BIG SISTER WHO WEARS GLASSES, EVERYTHING COULD LOOK LIKE THIS.

Many children and adults need to wear glasses, especially as they get older. Sometimes one of their eyes is stronger than the other, and sometimes vision is weak in both eyes. Some people see things better when they are close to them, which is called being *nearsighted*. Other people see things better when they are far away, which is called being *farsighted*.

IF YOU WERE AN ANT, EVERYTHING COULD LOOK LIKE THIS.

Ants see everything blurry compared to humans. And the smaller ants are, the blurrier things look! But ants' eyes are really good at detecting movement.

IF YOU WERE A GOAT, EVERYTHING COULD LOOK LIKE THIS.

Goats' eyes are really strange-looking to us humans. The pupils are rectangular! Scientists think the odd shape allows goats to keep an eye out, so to speak, for predators, which are other animals who might want to eat them. They also have panoramic vision, which means they can see far and wide.

IF YOU WERE A DRAGONFLY, EVERYTHING COULD LOOK LIKE THIS.

Dragonflies have huge compound eyes that contain around 30,000 teeny lenses giving them spectacular vision. They can actually see more color than we can. Even more unusual, they see in slow motion compared to humans. And believe it or not, dragonflies have nearly 360-degree vision, which means they can see in all directions at once. All these things make them excellent hunters!

IF YOU WERE A ROBIN, EVERYTHING COULD LOOK LIKE THIS.

Robins have amazingly sharp eyesight and can see worms from far away. Scientists think robins can sense the earth's magnetic field through their eyes, which helps them navigate. Also, robins can see a spectrum of colors that humans cannot.

IF YOU WERE A SMALL FISH, EVERYTHING COULD LOOK LIKE THIS.

Different fish have very different ways of seeing. Some see color, and some do not. Some see clearly, and some do not. It all depends on the species. And don't forget that seeing underwater is different from seeing things on land.

IF YOU WERE A WHALE, EVERYTHING COULD LOOK LIKE THIS.

Whales do not see color the way we do. They see the world in shades of gray, with lots of black thrown in. And with their eyes on the sides of their heads rather than in the middle as ours are, whales may see things very differently indeed!

IF YOU WERE AN EAGLE, EVERYTHING COULD LOOK LIKE THIS.

Eagles can see things better than humans can. They can see prey, which are animals they want to eat, such as mice, from very high up, and they see more colors than we do, even something called *ultraviolet light*. Eagles have the best vision of all creatures, as far as we know.

IF YOU WERE A MOUSE, EVERYTHING COULD LOOK LIKE THIS.

Mice are practically blind compared to human beings, but they have something we don't have—they can sense movement near them at night because of a special cell in their eyes. They also have whiskers that help them feel where they are going. Even though some of them have red eyes, mice are color-blind and can't see colors in the red family.

IF YOU WERE AN OWL, EVERYTHING COULD LOOK LIKE THIS.

Unlike humans, owls cannot move their eyes—but they make up for it! Instead of moving their eyes, owls turn their heads by as much as 270 degrees! And they have three eyelids to protect their eyes instead of just one. They also have very sharp vision for hunting, especially at night.

IF YOU WERE A RABBIT, EVERYTHING COULD LOOK LIKE THIS.

Rabbits have amazing vision. Their eyes are located on the sides of their heads, not in the front. This allows them to see almost 360 degrees, which means they can see what's behind them. You can never sneak up on a rabbit—it will always see you. Rabbit babies are born with their eyes closed. They open their eyes when they are ten days old.

IF YOU WERE A BEAVER, EVERYTHING COULD LOOK LIKE THIS.

Beavers don't have very good eyesight whether they are on land or swimming. But they do have something humans don't and it helps them see underwater. It's a clear membrane, or eyelid, that closes over their eyes when they swim. It's almost as if they're wearing goggles!

IF YOU WERE A WOLF, EVERYTHING COULD LOOK LIKE THIS.

Wolves have excellent vision, especially at night. Their vision is helped by a light-reflecting surface inside their eyes, while the outer part of their eyes can detect movement from far away. This helps them succeed as hunters. However, their eyesight is not as good as their sense of smell, which is almost 100 times better than humans'.

What does the world look like? It depends on who's looking.

And the wonderful thing is, it takes more than one set of eyes to get a full picture.

AUTHOR'S NOTE

One warm, sunny summer day, my grandson Kai and I were walking back to my house after a trip to the park. Kai and I like to talk as we walk, and that day we were talking about the things we saw around us—the flowers, the birds, the insects. We noticed some ants on the sidewalk and stopped for a minute to watch them. I said to Kai, "You must look like a giant to them!"

This conversation made me wonder what Kai and I looked like to the ants. I started to research how animals, birds and insects see. What I found out surprised, delighted and sometimes even shocked me. I didn't know that some species can see more colors than humans can or see ultraviolet light or simply see way better than we can. And I wondered, How do we know how animals see, since we can't see through their eyes?

The answer is science. Scientists use tools such as observation to deduce information. For instance, they may figure out how an animal's vision works by watching the animal and comparing the biology of its eye to the human eye. When scientists observe an eagle swooping down on prey from very high up in the sky, they conclude that the eagle must have very good eyesight to spot that mouse from so far away. And when they examine the eyes of a fish, they see that fish eyes aren't made the same way as human eyes. Our eyes have rods and cones that allow us to see. Fish don't have as many cones as humans do, and this means they don't see as well as we do. Scientists have all sorts of interesting methods of finding answers to the questions we have.

Maybe one day you will become a scientist and discover something new about how a different species sees!

Meanwhile, asking questions is the very best way to find things out, which is what Kai and I did.

See you on our next walk, Kai!

For Kai
with love
-C.M.

For my
curious mom
-C.L.

Published in Canada and the United States in 2022 by Orca Book Publishers.
orcabook.com

Library and Archives Canada Cataloguing in Publication
Title: Who's looking? : how animals see the world / Carol Matas; illustrated by Cornelia Li.
Other titles: Who is looking?
Names: Matas, Carol, 1949- author. | Li, Cornelia, illustrator.
Identifiers: Canadiana (print) 20210096578 | Canadiana (ebook) 20210096659 |
ISBN 9781459826762 (hardcover) | ISBN 9781459826779 (PDF) | ISBN 9781459826786 (EPUB)
Subjects: LCSH: Vision—Juvenile literature. | LCSH: Animals—Juvenile literature.
Classification: LCC QP475.7 .M38 2022 | DDC J573.8/8—dc23

Library of Congress Control Number: 2020951483

Summary: In this gorgeously illustrated nonfiction picture book, a young girl and her baby sister explore the land around them while various animals and insects look on. The art reflects the world as viewed by the animals, along with the text explaining some science behind each animal's unique type of vision.

Orca Book Publishers is committed to reducing the consumption of nonrenewable resources in the production of our books. We make every effort to use materials that support a sustainable future.

Orca Book Publishers gratefully acknowledges the support for its publishing programs provided by the following agencies: the Government of Canada, the Canada Council for the Arts and the Province of British Columbia through the BC Arts Council and the Book Publishing Tax Credit.

Artwork created with acrylic, ink and pencil, and digitally colored.

Cover and interior artwork by Cornelia Li
Edited by Liz Kemp
Design by Rachel Page

Printed and bound in Canada.

25 24 23 22 • 1 2 3 4